CHLOE *by* DESIGN

MADE
TO
Measure

BY MARGARET GUREVICH

ILLUSTRATIONS BY BROOKE HAGEL

STONE ARCH BOOKS
a capstone imprint

Chloe by Design is published by Stone Arch Books
A Capstone Imprint
1710 Roe Crest Drive
North Mankato, MN 56003
www.mycapstone.com

Library of Congress Cataloging-in-Publication Data

Names: Gurevich, Margaret, author. | Hagel, Brooke, illustrator. |
Gurevich, Margaret. Chloe by design. Title: Made to measure / by Margaret
Gurevich ; illustrations by Brooke Hagel.
Description: North Mankato, Minnesota : Stone Arch Books, a Capstone
imprint, [2016] | Series: Chloe by design |
Summary: Chloe and her mother take a trip to Los Angeles, where Chloe is
combining a guest appearance on the new season of Teen Design Diva, with
a tour of the Fashion Institute of Design and Merchandising, which is one
of the colleges that she is considering, aware that her mother would like
her to stay closer to Santa Cruz.
Identifiers: LCCN 2016008004| ISBN 9781496532626 (hardcover) | ISBN
9781496532664 (ebook pdf)
Subjects: LCSH: Fashion design--Juvenile fiction. | High school seniors--
Juvenile fiction. | High schools--Juvenile fiction. | Television game shows--
Juvenile fiction. | Mothers and daughters--Juvenile fiction. | Los Angeles
(Calif.)--Juvenile fiction. | Santa Cruz (Calif.)--Juvenile fiction. | CYAC:
Fashion design--Fiction. | High schools--Fiction. | Schools--Fiction. |
Reality television programs--Fiction. | Mothers and daughters--Fiction. |
Los Angeles (Calif.)--Fiction. | Santa Cruz (Calif.)--Fiction.
Classification: LCC PZ7.G98146 Mad 2016 | DDC 813.6--dc23
LC record available at http://lccn.loc.gov/2016008004

Designer: Alison Thiele
Editor: Alison Deering

Artistic Elements: Shutterstock

Printed and bound in China.
010388R

Measure twice, cut once
or you won't make the cut.

WITHDRAWN

Dear Diary,

It took almost a month of being back home, but I think things are finally coming together. I felt so behind when I first got back from New York. While I spent the summer working at Stefan Meyers and learning about the fashion industry, everyone else was touring colleges and thinking about applications. I had some *serious* culture shock when I came back to Santa Cruz. (Especially since my best friend Alex managed to make a bunch of new friends *and* get a new boyfriend while I was gone.) I spent a few weeks just blocking out the application process. Thankfully, Mimi, the owner of my favorite local boutique, helped me realize I needed to stop psyching myself out. I have to start researching and planning, or I'll never finish applications by January's deadlines.

Soooo . . . I looked up the requirements for FIT, FIDM, and Parsons — my top three choices — and started putting together my portfolio for each school. I'm also scheduling visits to the campuses. First up is FIDM in Los Angeles. I'm really lucky — I'm tying my visit in with guest judging for the current season of *Teen Design Diva*. Not only do I get to be a part of the show again, but the production team is also paying for my flight and hotel, which is a huge help.

(Touring schools that are all a plane ride away definitely adds up!) Honestly, though, I don't know where I'll end up. On the one hand, New York has always been my dream — I loved it there this summer, and Jake, my friend/crush, is there. But on the other hand, my friends and family are all in California . . .

Oh! I almost forgot to mention what else has been going on since my brain entered college mode. Winter Formal is in December, and Nina — more former frenemy — and I are designing some of the girls' dresses! The good news is that I can use the designs I'm creating in my college portfolios. The bad news is that they're *a lot* of work; everyone has a different idea of what they want, and it's up to me to make each vision into something wearable. I'm so excited to be designing again, and it's fun to imagine these dresses as the start of my own label — way in the future, I know! — but I'm hoping I didn't take on too much . . . Well, a car is here to take Mom and me to the airport for the LA trip. Wish me luck!

Xoxo — Chloe

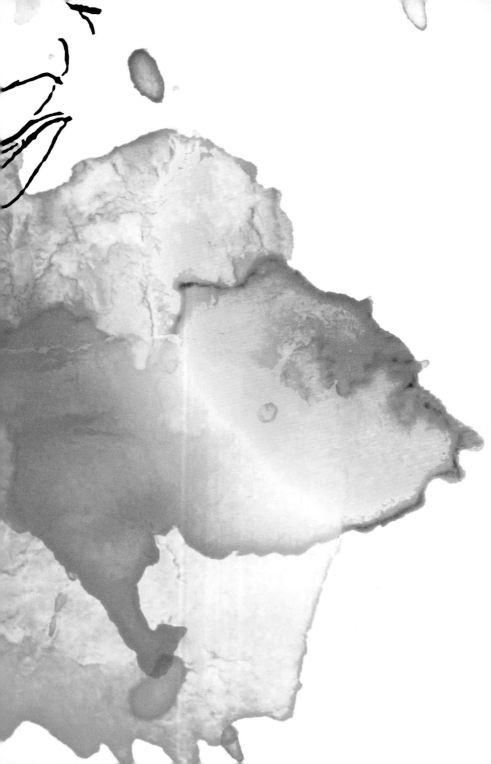

When my mom and I land in LA, the airport is a madhouse. But after my time in New York City, the noise and crowds don't bother me. In fact, the hustle and bustle is sort of comforting. I've missed this.

Mom shakes her head and smiles at me. "You look like you're actually enjoying the pushing and shoving." She grabs onto my sleeve as someone bumps into her.

"I better be careful, or I'll like it here," I say. I mean it as a joke, but it's the truth too. Part of me wants to like LA and FIDM, but there's another part of me that doesn't. Not liking it would make it easier because then I wouldn't have to choose between here and the schools in New York.

"Speaking of," Mom continues as she navigates us toward baggage claim, "please remind me what time our FIDM tour is."

I see a mom holding the hand of a toddler, which is obviously so the little boy doesn't get lost. As my mom grips my arm tighter, I smile. She's holding on to me so *she* doesn't get lost. The noise and crowds may make me excited, but they seem to make my mom nervous.

"Two o'clock," I say. "That's in three hours, which gives us time to get to our hotel, change clothes, and grab lunch."

The changing clothes part is key. I don't want to go on the college tour in my current outfit. The long-sleeved striped T-shirt, ripped jeans, and yellow sandals I'm wearing are fine for a plane ride and hanging out in an airport, but I'd like something a little more stylish for touring a fashion college.

Mom absently bites her nails, and I give her a hug. "Thanks for coming with me. I know this isn't exactly your scene."

Mom gives me a smile and loosens her grip on my arm. "I'd better get used to it. Whether it's here or in New York, this is clearly your thang."

I laugh at her choice of words. "Um, my *what?*"

Mom blushes. "Isn't that what you kids say?"

"Not really," I say, still giggling as I grab our suitcases off the carousel. My mom has always been so supportive of everything I've done. I'm really going to miss her, no matter which college I go to.

I must be staring at her because Mom says, "What? Are you trying to get over how uncool I am?"

I smile at her. "No, nothing like that. I'm just thinking about how lucky I am to have you."

* * *

"This is more my speed," Mom says as we relax at an outdoor table at a café near FIDM. Even though it's in the middle of the city, it somehow doesn't attract city noise. Or maybe it's just an illusion created by the restaurant's soft décor and the oversized umbrellas shading each table and shielding us from the other patrons as well as city traffic.

"I read about this place in one of my magazines," I say, grabbing a breadstick out of a breadbasket lined with pink paper. "Celebrities like to come here because of the privacy."

"Perfect for you, then," Mom says with a wink. "You need to keep the paparazzi at bay."

I laugh. "Please. I think my fifteen minutes are up." Although since we have our interview after this, I *am* dressed to impress in a white, open-weave sweater, faux-leather shorts, and black flats.

Just then, a waiter approaches our table. He stares at us for a few beats, seeming nervous, before speaking. "Um, I'm Jeff," he says. "I'll be taking your order."

LOS ANGELES
TRAVEL
Design

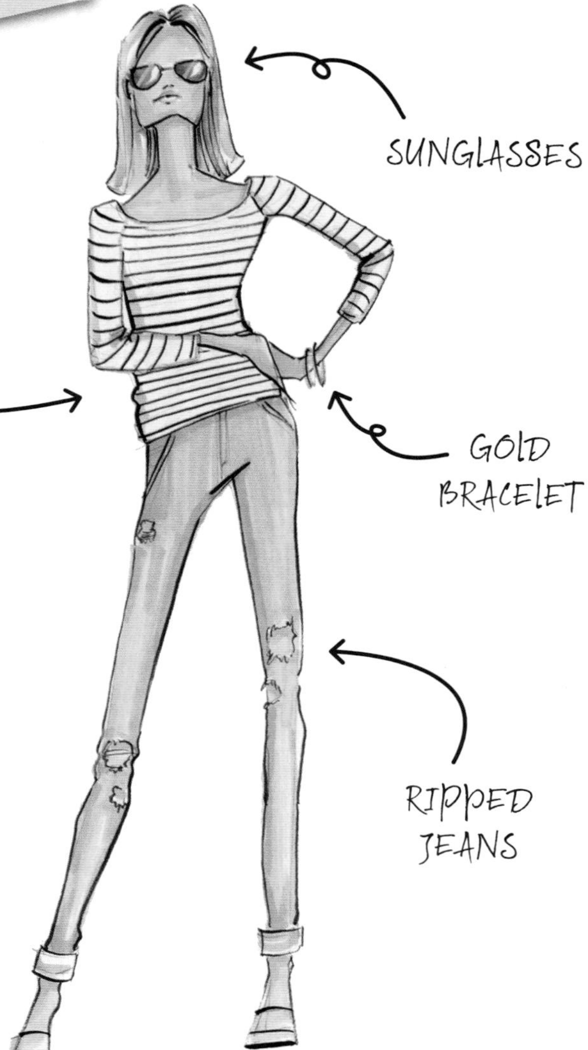

CM CM CM

SUNGLASSES

STRIPED
LONG-SLEEVED
T-SHIRT

GOLD
BRACELET

YELLOW
SANDALS

RIPPED
JEANS

FIDM
CAMPUS TOUR
Design
OFF-THE-SHOULDER NECKLINE
OPEN-WEAVE SWEATER
FAUX-LEATHER SHORTS
Dressed to Impress
BLACK BALLET FLATS
• Arrive in LA
• Go to hotel
• Change clothes
• Grab lunch
• College tour

"Hi Jeff," says my mom warmly. "We'll both be having the turkey paninis with a side of arugula and goat cheese salad."

Jeff writes the order down, avoiding eye contact. "Anything to drink?" he asks.

"A pink lemonade for each of us," I say.

Jeff looks up at me, then quickly back at his pad of paper. "Thank you," he mumbles before going back inside the restaurant.

"Do I have a sesame seed stuck in my teeth or something?" I ask my mom, smiling wide.

"Nope. I just think you're wrong about your fifteen minutes being up," she replies. "He probably recognizes you from *Teen Design Diva*."

I wave my hand dismissively. "This is LA. There are way bigger celebs here." To prove my point, I glance around the restaurant, but I can't see who's who beneath any of the pastel-colored umbrellas.

Mom shrugs. "True, but reality shows are hot. Plus your face is still memorable thanks to your guest judging appearance on *Teen Design Diva* this past season. The producers wouldn't ask you to guest judge again if they didn't think it would be good for the show's ratings."

I groan. I have mixed feelings about my celebrity status. On the one hand, the guest judging and all the opportunities

I've been given are amazing. But worrying about how I was portrayed while on the show was less than awesome. When *Teen Design Diva* first aired, our school and town were abuzz about Nina and me. I was glad all that died down this year.

"Your salads and paninis," says our waiter, coming back to our table. The plates rattle a little as he sets them down on the pink tablecloth.

"Thank you," I say, smiling.

The server lingers, and I feel weird eating while he's still there. Finally he takes a deep breath and moves closer to our table. "Here's the thing," he whispers after a quick glance behind him, "I'm not allowed to do this, but my girlfriend's birthday is tomorrow. She's a huge fan and loved all your designs on *Design Diva*. She wants to be a designer too. Any chance I can have your autograph? I'd win the prize for best boyfriend ever."

"Sure," I say with a smile. "No problem. I'll sketch something and sign it for her before we go."

"Thanks so much!" With that he hurries off to wait on another table.

My mom gives me an *I-told-you-so* look. "As I was saying . . ."

"Yeah, yeah." I bite into my sandwich, feeling happy and flattered. Sometimes being recognized isn't so bad after all.

"Welcome to FIDM!" our perky tour guide says later that afternoon. "My name is Claire, and I'm a senior. Today, I'll be your eyes and ears for everything FIDM. If you have any questions, feel free to ask."

My mom and I — along with a dozen or so prospective students and their parents — are gathered at FIDM's campus entrance. The white buildings serve as a good contrast to the green and red shrubs and grassy area situated before them. If a campus could feel fashion-forward, that's how I'd describe this one.

Claire's outfit doesn't disappoint, either. She's paired a loose white cami with black stretchy jeans and black ankle boots. A red leather jacket adds a pop of color and fun accessories complete her look.

TOUR GUIDE
OUTFIT
Design

WHITE
PLEATED
CAMI

RED
LEATHER
JACKET

BLACK
SKINNY
JEANS

BLACK
BOOTIES

"This is the main reception area," Claire continues, leading us into a room with art deco style carpet, muted lighting, and comfy-looking furniture. The students sitting on the couches and chairs are playing on their phones or sketching. In the middle of the room is a mannequin dressed in a patterned shift dress.

"Even the reception area is fashionable," I whisper to my mom. Just like that, I can picture myself here. It's silly because I've only seen the courtyard and this one room, but for once, I let myself enjoy the feeling and push the what-ifs out of my head.

"What I love most about FIDM is the atmosphere," Claire tells the group. A group of students walks by, and Claire gives them a discreet wave. "You're so close to all the entertainment and fashion events, and that excitement transfers to the building and the classes."

A girl wearing loose peach-colored jogger pants and a black-and-white sweater raises her hand. "Um, how do you focus on school here? It seems so fun and exciting."

Claire laughs. "I felt the same way when I first started here, but you get used to it. Even as a senior, I find this place amazing. But you remember why you came here, which is to be a designer, and you put the fun to the side."

The girl nods, but her face tells me she's not convinced.

"Let's keep walking," says Claire. "The classrooms are up next."

The classrooms are just as cool as the reception area. Everything is brightly colored, and there are several mannequins stationed around the room for the students to work on too. If we had these kinds of classrooms at my school in Santa Cruz, no one would ever complain about going to class.

The other prospective students in the group whisper things like "cool" and "awesome," and Claire says, "The goal of FIDM's classes is not only to teach but to inspire as well."

Okay, that sounds totally cheesy and like something all the tour guides have to say, but it seems true too. Unlike in my school, I don't see anyone in the class playing on his or her phone or hiding behind a book to take a nap. They're all listening to the teacher and cutting and measuring and *smiling*.

"How long are classes?" asks a boy on the tour.

"Each one is three hours long," says Claire. "And carrying a muslin, tote bag, textbooks, and a tool kit to each one can be a pain. You have to plan so you're not late to class."

Three hours? I think. *Sheesh!* The classrooms may look fun, but that's a long time. And, if I'm going to carry all that stuff, I need to start working out now so I don't hurt myself!

Claire leads the group out of the classroom and back down the hall. "These window displays," she says, pointing to a glass case with a dressed mannequin, "are all done by students."

The current mannequin is wearing a strapless multicolored dress. It has a sweetheart neckline and looks like it's made of flowers. I imagine one of my designs showcased like this for everyone to see. It'd be a dream come true.

"Another amazing thing about FIDM is our museum. It's open to the public and totally free," says Claire.

"Unlike this school," a dad in the group jokes.

Claire looks at him and nods. "You're right. This school has so much to offer. The fact that it's so close to the movie and television industry in LA allows FIDM to bring in terrific industry professionals. We also have a great alumni program, and most of our students get jobs after graduation, but this is an expensive school." She looks around and lowers her voice. "There is a lot of opportunity here, but if you're comparing it to some other fashion schools, the price is more than double."

My heart sinks. We're still working out how to pay for transportation to NYC for my FIT and Parsons tours, and that's just two plane tickets. College tuition will cost way more.

My mom looks at my sad face and then at Claire. "But you have programs that can help here, right? Financial aid and things like that?"

"Yes! Definitely." Claire looks relieved that my mom mentioned this. "The financial aid office is a great resource, and we offer scholarships. And students can also work to help pay for their education."

Hearing Claire's assurances makes me feel a little better. I didn't plan on working while I was in college, but it could be an option.

Claire seems eager to change topics to something less stressful. "Let's walk to the museum next," she suggests. "The current exhibit showcases designs from Emmy-nominated shows."

When we enter the museum, I immediately think of all the fashion and entertainment magazines Alex, my best friend, and I read. She would love this place. I even recognize a few dresses from my favorite shows. One is from a creepy series Alex and I watch called *Beneath the Ground*. It takes place in an alternate universe, and the characters wear Victorian-inspired clothing.

I recognize a dress from last season's finale. It's a red-and-white Georgian style gown in cotton and satin with a matching choker. I take out my sketchpad and do a quick drawing so I don't forget the small details. I want to try and sketch a more modern version when I get home. Out of the corner of my eye, I notice two other students on the tour doing the same. It might sound cheesy, but this makes me feel connected to them and this place even more.

"Our last stop," Claire announces, "is the annex." She leads us back outside to where our tour began. This time we go past the courtyard and enter through the side of the building. "You might recognize this *pool* from our brochures, but it's not really a pool."

I move closer to it. This close, it's easy to see that the pool isn't filled with water after all — it's a sunken area covered with blue mats for lounging and studying. The *pool* is surrounded by a raised platform with laptop-equipped lounge chairs. It's easily the coolest study area I've ever seen.

"Who can see themselves sitting and sketching on these chairs?" Claire asks. We all raise our hands. "Then I've done my job," she says with a smile. "It was great meeting all of you, and I hope you'll apply."

When Claire leaves, my mother and I sit side-by-side on the lounge chairs. There are students around, but they don't seem to mind us being here.

"So what do you think?" Mom asks. "Do you like it?"

I nod, still in awe. "I do. How can you not?"

"Even I wanted to go here," Mom says with a laugh.

MATCHING
CHOKER
NECKLACE

FIDM
MUSEUM
Sketches

GEORGIAN
STYLE

TASSEL
CLUTCH

- Victorian-inspired
- Alternate universe
- Creepy TV series
- "Beneath the Ground"

RED
EMBROIDERY

COTTON &
SATIN

"It's way more expensive than FIT, though," I say.

Mom nods, and I'm glad she doesn't try to sugarcoat anything. "That's something you'll have to think about. If you went here, you'd most likely have to do the work-study program, which might be hard while you're studying."

"True," I say. "Can we maybe think more about that later? Like after I've seen the New York schools? I just want to pretend anything is possible for a little while longer."

Mom smiles. "Sure," she says. "I think you deserve that."

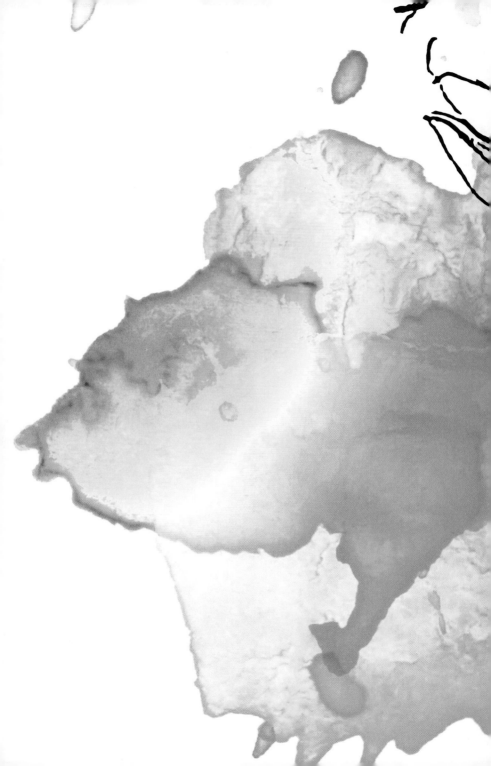

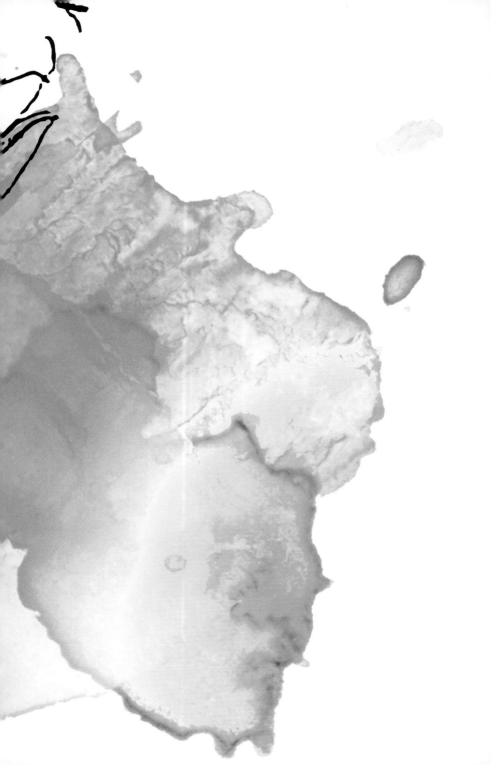

When Monday — the day of my *Teen Design Diva* gig — rolls around, I can tell my mom is glad it's our last day in Los Angeles. The rest of the weekend flew by, and I could happily stay here longer, but the LA noise and activity has been getting to Mom. She needs a break. She says it's even worse than New York.

I kind of get what she's saying. There seems to be more car congestion and traffic here. I'm fine with it, though. Thankfully Mom will have the day to take it easy. She'll be spending the day at a cute bookstore she found. It even has a small nook where customers can curl up on cushions and read.

While Mom is resting, I'll be in the conference room on the top floor of our hotel acting as guest judge. Just like during my time at *Teen Design Diva*, the producers are using the hotel to not only house the contestants but also as the workroom and studio for the competition. I wish I knew the theme of today's challenge ahead of time so I could mentally prepare, but I'm guessing they want me to approach the task with fresh eyes.

Since I don't have to be on set for judging for another two hours, I have plenty of time to kill. I start by flipping through the full-color coffee table book in our room. It shows the hotel as it was in its early years, and how it was finally completed in 1925.

Even though it's been updated since then, the current owners have kept key pieces from the original building, like signed photos of famous movie stars. The hotel and our room have a very old-style Hollywood feel. Much of the décor is done in shades of burgundy and gold. Even the walls are burgundy. White moldings form a frame around the ceiling, and decorative gold swirls accent the corners.

I finish flipping through the book and still have plenty of time before I'm due upstairs, so I decide to head down to the lobby. The décor reminds me of the red carpet premieres I've seen on television. There are even velvet ropes in front of the check-in desk, and the walls are covered with black-and-white photos of old movies and movie stars.

I spot an armchair that's off to a corner and sit on it to sketch. I imagine the many people who have passed through this hotel in the past. A woman in a wide hat approaches the front desk to ask about good places to eat. She's wearing a yellow, knee-length dress with a ruffle on the bottom and red pumps. I pull out my sketchbook and do a quick drawing of her outfit. Her retro look would fit in perfectly with my vision of how the hotel would have looked back in the 1920s.

I like how she's dressed but play with the design to transform it into something a bit more modern, making it my own. Rather than a feminine dress, I draw a cool, modern jumpsuit, keeping the bright, bold yellow the same on both designs. I sketch quickly, adding a cowl neckline and loose, drapey pants. I imagine the jumpsuit in a luxurious fabric like satin. Paired with a bold lip and a fun, feathered clutch, it would be the perfect outfit for a night out.

I look at the two drawings side-by-side — the retro version and my modern twist — and wonder if there's a way to add this to my portfolio. All the schools I'm applying to have different requirements, and while this doesn't match any of them exactly, maybe I can make it work.

STRAPLESS
SWEETHEART
BODICE

FEATHER
CLUTCH

YELLOW
KNEE-LENGTH
DRESS

RUFFLE
HEM

PANTS &
CAMISOLE
COMBO

RED
SHOES

ORIGINAL
LA HOTEL
Design

I smile. It's been a while since I sketched something just for the sake of sketching. Lately it feels like my portfolio is the only reason I pick up my pencils and sketchpad. It's nice to have it be an afterthought rather than the *reason* I'm designing.

I realize that's one reason this whole college application process has been stressing me out so much. In the past, any time I've been upset, anxious, or overwhelmed, all I had to do was take out my sketchpad and draw something. By the time I was done, the bad feelings would have lessened or disappeared altogether, and I'd be able to face whatever lay ahead.

These days, though, the college clock is ticking, and since each sketch is a portfolio necessity, there hasn't been time to be creative on my own terms. It's been hard to fit in drawing for the sake of drawing. Designing is something I've always loved, but lately it's become work.

I check the clock. The producers don't need me upstairs for another thirty minutes, but I know how cranky Jasmine — one of the *Design Diva* judges — can get when she thinks people are running late. It won't hurt to get there a little early.

I close my sketchpad, feeling lighter than I have in weeks. I remember how stressful being a *Teen Design Diva* contestant was. Maybe part of my role today will be to remind the designers not to forget why they wanted to be on the show in the first place. After all, it never hurts to have a reminder that what someone else thinks shouldn't stop you from following your dream.

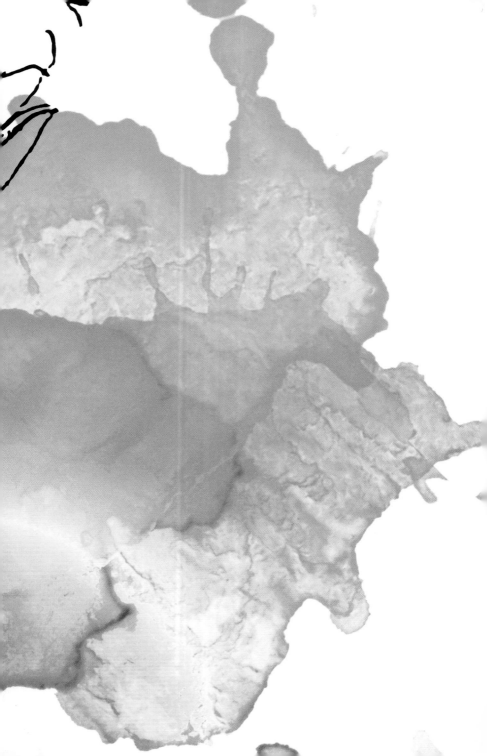

"There she is!" Missy, one of the *Design Diva* judges, exclaims as soon as I open the door to the conference room.

I had expected the room to have the same vintage feel as the rest of the hotel, but it looks more like a huge office. Even the carpeting is a drab, dark blue. The plus side is that there is tons of space for the design contestants to stretch out material and work. That's more important than a pretty space.

"Chic as usual," says Jasmine, giving me air kisses on both cheeks.

"Thanks," I say. I try to keep my voice light and casual, so it doesn't give away the fact that this is the third outfit I tried on before deciding it was the one. I always feel extra pressure to look good during *Design Diva* tapings. First, there's the need to impress the judges. Then, I feel like I have to make a good impression on the contestants. If I don't look like I know what I'm doing as a designer, they'll ignore what I have to say. Last, there's the whole being on television thing.

I once read an article about the dos and don'ts of television appearances, and it gave a whole rundown of best colors to wear. White can make you look too bright, while black can make you look washed out. Patterns appear to vibrate on the screen, and red is a no-no because it bleeds into the screen. Pastels are best.

It was *a lot* of rules to follow, but I worked hard to find the best outfit that was *me* but also worked on screen. The winner was a light blue chambray top with pink jeans. Metallic heels add some pizzazz.

"Good to see you, Chloe," Hunter, the other judge, greets me. "We have an interesting challenge ahead of us today. Any guesses as to what it'll be?"

I look around the room for clues. There are sewing machines, mannequins, and rolls of fabric in place. The fabric runs the gamut from solid pastels to prints to bright neon. Even with my experience as a contestant on the show and as a guest judge over the summer, there's still no way to know. The task could be anything. But I know the challenges tend to run in the non-traditional direction.

"Clothing inspired by your favorite prehistoric era?" I guess blindly.

Missy laughs. "Not even we are that out there. Although, maybe we should be."

I think she's kidding at first, but then she takes out a notepad and jots something down.

"I'll give you a hint," Jasmine says. "It has to do with this hotel."

Of course! That would totally make sense. The judges always have a reason for what they do. When I was on *Teen Design Diva*, one task involved cupcakes that were wheeled into the colorful hotel lobby.

"Hollywood-inspired designs?" I guess, thinking of the old Hollywood feel I picked up on earlier.

"Close," Hunter says. "Movie-inspired designs."

"Ooh, that is fun! And much better than the challenge I had to do with Nina that involved using stuff from the hardware store."

Hunter chuckles. "We felt bad about that — kind of. Speaking of Nina, have you seen her around?"

"We're actually kind of friendly. Weird, right?"

Missy raises an eyebrow. "A little, but promise me that when the two of you open your own boutique one day, you'll credit the show for bringing you ladies together."

Now it's my turn to laugh. "I promise. But I don't see that happening."

Just then the doors open, and the contestants start filing in. Is it my imagination or do they look older than the group I competed with? They don't look scared or nervous. I notice no one is hamming for the cameras, either. These contestants look so serious.

"How long have you been taping?" I ask Hunter.

"We're more than halfway done already," he says. "Today, we're narrowing the eight contestants down to six."

That means they're only one task away from the top five. At this point, the contestants probably know what to expect. They've probably also realized that even if they do their best, there's no telling what the judges will say.

"What's this group like?" I whisper.

"Very mature," says Missy. "But also very no-nonsense. And they talk back a lot."

"That must be frustrating," I say.

"Sometimes," Missy says, shrugging. "But it makes for good television, and isn't that the point?"

I thought the point was to be the best designer you could be, but I keep that thought to myself.

Jasmine waits for everyone to get settled down. Then, she snaps her fingers and says, "Welcome!"

A girl in a blue baseball cap and overalls actually rolls her eyes. If Jasmine sees this, she ignores it. I look around the room. Some of the designers have their eyes on Jasmine, while others are focused on the floor. A guy in a green fedora and paisley shirt is moving his fingers at his side like he's playing air guitar. A guy in jeans and work boots is scowling at a girl with her hair in braids. Her long-sleeved tee with the word *FOOTBALL* in the center and black jeans with holes at the knees make me smile. The outfit reminds me of something Alex would have worn once upon a time. She smirks at the guy staring at her, and he scowls and turns away.

"First," Jasmine continues, "let me introduce our guest judge for the day, Chloe Montgomery, the first *Teen Design Diva* winner."

Pigtails Girl smiles at me. Fedora Guy stops playing his imaginary guitar and gives me a look of approval. Baseball Cap girl rolls her eyes again. At least she's consistent. Some of the contestants clap, while the rest look like they couldn't care less that I'm here. Maybe they don't.

The reaction makes me nervous, like I have to prove myself once again. I know it's silly. I'm just here to help; I don't have to put on some show. But I can't help it. Maybe it's the all-too-familiar environment, but it's like I'm back on the show as a contestant again and stuck trying to make people believe I belong.

Hunter motions to a box wrapped in gold paper that's sitting on a nearby table. "You will each pick a slip of paper from this box," he says. "It will tell you a movie title. Your job will be to create an outfit inspired by the movie you've chosen. Volunteers to go first?"

Baseball Cap waves her hand in the air. For a change, she's alert and interested.

"Tina, come on up," Hunter says to the girl.

Tina runs up, closes her eyes, and puts her hand into the box. "*101 Dalmatians*," she says with a sigh. And it's back to sullen eye rolling.

"Can I go next?" the girl with pigtails asks.

"Here you go, Lexi," says Hunter, shaking the box.

"*The Wizard of Oz*!" Lexi says, clapping her hands.

Fedora Guy — whose name turns out to be Peter — gets *Finding Neverland*, which I think is a good fit. Work Boots — also known as Lee — gets *Men in Black*. The other movies picked are *The Devil Wears Prada*, *Star Wars*, *The Sound of Music*, and *Father of the Bride*.

"You have three hours," Jasmine announces once all the movies are picked. "You may begin."

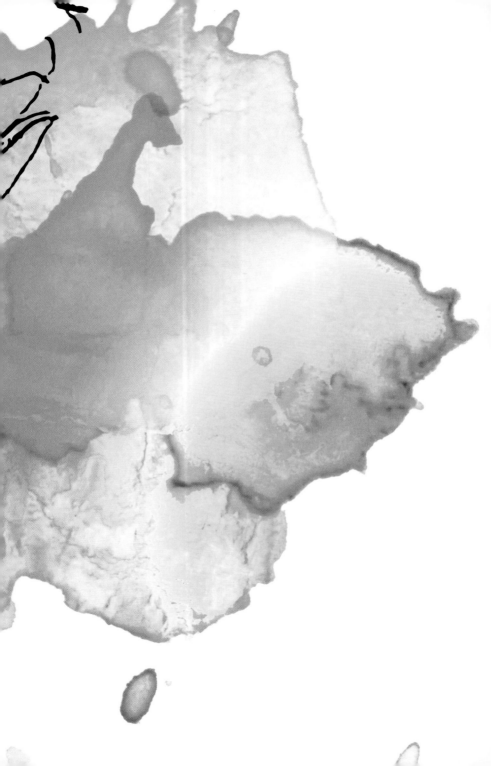

I expect the contestants to make a mad dash for the fabric and sewing machines, but instead they all take out their sketchpads and start drawing.

"Wow," I say. "That's not how everyone reacted during my season."

Missy shrugs. "I guess that's what happens when they've seen two seasons of the show and kind of know what to expect."

"The designs are less entertaining," says Jasmine, pouting.

"Not good television, huh?" I tease.

"Exactly," says Missy.

The first hour is a little boring with the contestants all sketching and measuring. Just when I think they're cutting it close, they start to gather fabric. Lee starts with black and metallic fabrics, and Peter picks green tulle and lace. Vicki, who got *Star Wars*, chooses muted colors like browns and khakis. Other contestants are clearly going for something a little more glamorous based on the lace, satin, and embellishments they've chosen.

I walk around and am impressed with how quickly the designers are able to sew. I notice Vicki make a mistake with her stitching, but she quickly rips the thread and fixes the problem. The designers use their mannequins efficiently too, draping fabric, measuring there, cutting here, and adjusting the results — all within minutes.

I walk up to Peter and watch him make a belt with the leather, velvet, and gold clasp. Then he uses a sheer fabric to create what looks like a bodice.

"When I saw you choose the materials, I was thinking Peter Pan," I say.

"That would have been too cutesy given my name," he says. "And too obvious given the film. I wanted something a little girlier too since this is my little sister's favorite movie."

"That's really sweet," I say. "Good job so far."

I walk up to Lee. His *Men in Black* inspired design is less than endearing. I love metallic fabrics, but I'm not sure what he's trying to do.

"Can you tell me about your piece?" I ask him.

"Not really," he says. "I mean not now. I don't like to give away what's behind the genius. Trust me, though, you'll be amazed."

"I'll wait to be awed," I say, trying not to laugh as I move on to the other contestants.

The ones that interest me the most are the designs inspired by *The Sound of Music* and *The Devil Wears Prada*. When I pass Nancy, the designer for *The Sound of Music* style, she's working on a white peplum dress. I'm about to ask her more about it, but think about what Lee said and decide that being surprised is not a bad thing.

I move over to Becca's *The Devil Wears Prada* design. It's a little hard to figure out. The fitted sleeveless top has a large bow at the collar that looks odd.

"I'm working on the sleeves," Becca tells me through a mouthful of pins.

"Can't wait to see," I say. I hurry away, afraid she'll choke on the pins if I keep talking with her. I walk around the other designs and wonder which one the judges will like the most.

"One hour!" Hunter announces, but no one seems fazed or hurried.

My phone vibrates, and I look down to see a text from Jake McKay. Jake is . . . well, I don't really know how to describe him. We're friends but maybe a little more than that. We met at the start of summer — pre-*Design Diva*. He lives in New York City, which means I don't get to see him much, but we still talk and text regularly.

I know Jake wants to hear how my FIDM tour went, especially since I told him about my application anxiety last week, but there's a reason I haven't texted him yet. I don't want to tell him that it went great, and I'm loving LA, especially since I know he's hoping I'll come back to New York for college. I'll have to talk to him soon, but not now. At this moment, I need to keep my head in this room.

Just then Hunter calls, "Thirty minutes," and the cameramen converge on the contestants and their designs. Even though the contestants' faces don't show much emotion, I notice beads of sweat on their foreheads. I also see them wring their hands, bite their nails, and play with their hair — all signs they're just as nervous as I was during the judging process.

Hunter, Jasmine, Missy, and I do one last lap around the room. The contestants' attention shifts from their fabric to the clock and back to the fabric as they all hurry to put the finishing touches on their designs.

"I love this last-minute tension," Jasmine says, rubbing her hands.

I frown. "I don't. Their anxiety is actually rubbing off on me. I totally get what they're going through."

"That's why we have you here, Chloe," says Missy. "I used to be the softie, but I'm afraid I've gotten tougher. You help balance things out."

I frown slightly. I guess that's a compliment.

Hunter laughs. "Ignore them. You're just more humane. Like me." But then, in a loud, booming voice that makes me jump, he shouts: "Time's up!"

So much for softer and more humane.

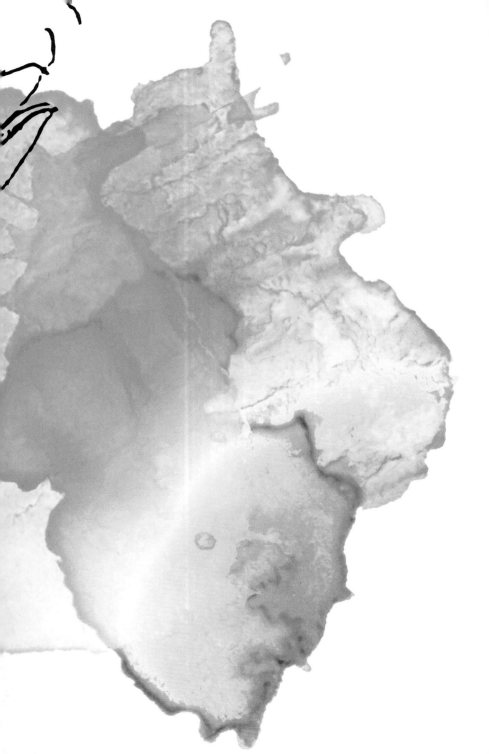

6

"Lee," says Hunter once all the contestants have gathered in the center of the room with their mannequins, "we'll begin with you. Tell us about your piece."

"Well," Lee starts, "the guys in *Men in Black* were secret government agents, so I thought it would be fun to put a spin on their boring black suits. I chose to create a more modern, feminine version." He points to his fitted vest and loose, ankle-length pants. "I also added a metallic tank underneath to give it a futuristic vibe."

"When you said to trust you," I say, "I didn't think you'd come up with a design that's so put-together. Nice job."

Lee gives a slight bow and looks relieved. Vicki's *Star Wars* design is next, and the judges look at each other warily.

CONTESTANT
MOVIE-INSPIRED
Designs

KHAKI
TENT
DRESS

BECCA'S
*THE DEVIL WEARS
PRADA DRESS*

MODERN &
FEMININE
SUITING

BOW
COLLAR,
SWEATER,
& STRIPED
SKIRT

LEE'S
*MEN IN BLACK
SUIT*

VICKI'S
*STAR WARS
DRESS*

"What's your inspiration for this?" Missy finally asks.

Vicki straightens the khaki fabric. "It's a tent dress, modeled after the clothes the little furry Ewoks wore in the *Star Wars* movie. It gives it a modern spin, don't you think?"

Jasmine purses her lips. "It looks a little shapeless to me."

"I'm really sorry, Vicki, but I have to agree," says Hunter. "A tent dress can look modern and stylish, but it looks like you just pieced the fabric together without really doing measurements."

I want to say something positive, but they're right. There's no definition, and I wonder how this even took her three hours to make.

Fortunately, I'm saved from speaking when Vicki steps back, and the judges call Becca forward. Her finished outfit is glaringly different from what I saw before. The added sleeves complement the bow collar, and she's paired her top with a striped skirt for contrast.

I shoot Becca a discreet thumbs-up, and she smiles. Jasmine makes a few suggestions about better stitching, but even she's stumped to give any other criticism. Lucky for Jasmine, Tina's Cruella De Vil-inspired dress gives Jasmine and the other judges plenty to discuss.

"Notice the contrast of black and white," Tina says, pointing to her dress, which is half-black and half-white.

"The jagged asymmetrical hem is a nod to Cruella's villainous spirit."

"And the high, spiky collar is for the villainous spirit too, I assume?" says Hunter.

"That's correct," says Tina.

"Here's where I'm struggling," says Missy. "The stitching is perfect and professional. The difficulty of the design is impressive too. But I'm just not feeling this dress. It's so over the top."

I think about my goal of keeping the contestants inspired and telling them to stay true to themselves. I open my mouth to say this when Tina stomps her foot.

"Your opinions aren't law, you know," she snaps. "Maybe you just don't get creativity."

Missy grits her teeth. "Our opinions may not be law," she says. "But they decide your fate here."

Tina turns her back to us, and Hunter sighs. "Moving on," he says.

Bubbly Lexi barely lets Missy get the first syllable of her name out before she launches into the description of her Glinda-inspired dress. "For the bodice, I made a plunging V-neck of gathered silk crepe. This is draped into a wide, gathered waistband with an organza bolero jacket," says Lexi.

"It's really lovely," I say. "You did a beautiful job on the skirt as well."

"Thank you," says Lexi. "I imagined Glinda's dramatic entrance and was trying to mimic that drama with the yards of organza gathered and pintucked into a skirt."

"This makes me want to see the movie all over again," says Missy.

"I'm just glad you didn't do anything wizard- or munchkin-inspired," Jasmine adds.

"Thank you guys so much," gushes Lexi.

"Two more to go," says Hunter. "Peter, you're up."

"Yes, so as I was telling Chloe, I have a sister who loves all things Peter Pan, so she was my inspiration for this dress," says Peter. "She loves lace, flowers, and ruffles, so I included all of those elements in my design."

"The flowers fit beautifully with the tulle," I say.

"And I like its romantic quality," Hunter adds.

Peter grins. "Thank you."

"Finally," says Hunter, "we have Scott with his *Father of the Bride* design."

When I see Scott's finished design I'm both surprised and impressed. I'd never match his design with his current style. Unlike the Yankees jersey, baggy shorts, and high-top sneakers he's wearing, his dress design is both fun and elegant.

"Seems like sisters are the theme today," says Scott. "Mine just got engaged and wanted me to design her wedding dress. The movie I got was like, crazy coincidence."

"Totally," says Hunter. "Why the two-piece?"

"My sister isn't super formal, so I wanted something more off-beat but still elegant. I think I did that with the full skirt and lace halter top," says Scott.

"I agree," says Missy. "I hope she likes it."

"Thank you all," says Hunter. "We will let you know our thoughts soon."

As the contestants get a breather, the judges and I head into another room to discuss the designs, although there's not much to discuss. Our favorites are Becca's *The Devil Wears Prada* design, Nancy's *The Sound of Music* inspired dress, Peter's *Finding Neverland* design, Scott's *Father of the Bride* two-piece wedding ensemble, and Lexi's *The Wizard of Oz* Glinda-inspired gown. That leaves Tina's Cruella-inspired dress, Lee's *Men in Black* suit, and Vicki's *Star Wars* sack — I mean dress.

"Well," says Jasmine, "I think we can all agree we have to let Vicki go. That leaves Lee or Tina."

"Tina's was definitely more inspired than Lee's," says Hunter, "but —"

I interrupt. "She's kind of rude, and it seems like she doesn't really want to get better if it means messing with her vision." I learned a lot from my experience on *Teen*

Design Diva and during my internship. It's important to stay true to yourself, but you also have to be willing to see that there might be a better way to do things.

"Exactly," says Hunter. "I'm sure she'll go places, but she's been giving us attitude from day one. This experience is about learning, and it's clear she doesn't think we have anything to teach her."

"I completely agree," Jasmine says, "but every show needs a villain."

"I hear you, Jazz," says Missy, "but I've had enough of her too. At least Lee will take direction, and I know he'll create something more daring next time. We have a situation here where both are talented. I'd rather talk with Lee again."

Jasmine sighs. "You're right, I know. She's gotten on my last nerve too."

"So it's decided," says Hunter.

We all nod and head back in to break the news to the designers. As the producers and cameras get into position for the elimination, I brace myself for Tina's reaction, doubting it will be pretty.

At least it'll be good preparation, I think. Because I'll soon have to tell Jake my own bad news — that after seeing FIDM, I'm not so sure FIT is my only dream school anymore.

CONTESTANT
MOVIE-INSPIRED
Designs

PETER'S
FINDING NEVERLAND
DRESS

FLOWER
CROWN

LACE
HALTER
TOP

FULL
TAFFETA
SKIRT

FLOWER
DETAILS

GREEN
TULLE &
LACE

GATHERED
SKIRT

OFF-BEAT
& ELEGANT

SCOTT'S
FATHER OF THE BRIDE
DRESS

"What do you mean you haven't told Jake yet?" Alex asks as we walk through the mall back home later that week.

I admit, I'm kind of being a coward. I've been back in Santa Cruz for three days, and so far all I've told Jake about FIDM is that it was "okay." And even that was through texts.

"I just know he'll be bummed if I tell him how much I liked it," I say. "It's the kind of conversation you want to have with someone in person, you know?"

"True, but when is that happening?" Alex asks. "You can't avoid him forever."

"This weekend, apparently. Liesel is having a fashion show in Santa Cruz, and he's flying in to help her."

"And you just found out?" asks Alex.

"I guess it was a last-minute decision," I reply. "Jake wanted to surprise me, but I guess he could tell something was up, so he told me."

"Geez, Chloe, cheer up. It's not the end of the world," Alex says. "First of all, you know Jake just wants you to be happy. Second of all, as much as I'd love for you to choose FIDM, you're still going to tour Parsons and FIT. Who knows what'll happen?"

I give Alex a hug. She always knows what to say. "You're right. My FIDM visit made me feel better about this whole college thing. I feel less out of the loop now. I mean, I'm still no closer to making a decision, but at least it's a start."

"Exactly," Alex agrees. "And in the meantime, we can focus on more fun stuff — like looking for clothes."

We walk into a store that's more Alex's style than mine, but shopping is shopping. I can't complain. After all, a year ago I would have had to drag Alex to the mall.

"What do you think of this?" Alex asks, holding up a knee-length dress with thick peach and white stripes. "Maybe with my brown suede ankle boots?"

"I love that," I agree, marveling at how far Alex's style has come. "You just need the right accessories." I spot a long, gold chain on a jewelry rack and hold it up against the dress. "What do you think?"

"Oh, I love that. You have such a good eye for these things." Alex tosses the dress over her arm and flips through some more hangers.

I smile. "Thanks. It kind of reminds me of going through the racks during my internship. I had to see what went together, why people liked it, stuff like that. Jake went on one of those trips with me. Can't say he loved it, though."

While I'm thinking about him, I decide to text him. I take out my phone and type: *Thinking of you while rack shopping!*

Jake writes back in seconds. *Like in NYC. I'd totally suffer through it again if it meant we could hang out.*

"He's so sweet," Alex says when I show her the text. "You guys will make it work, wherever you go."

"I hope so. But that reminds me — I still need to find a way to pay for my flight to New York. Too bad they're not taping another season of *Design Diva* there," I joke.

"Your dad travels for business," Alex says. "Maybe he has frequent flyer miles or something."

"Maybe," I say, but I'm not as optimistic as Alex about it.

"Well, if there's one thing you've shown me, Chloe Montgomery, it's how hard you work at something you want," Alex says with a grin.

I laugh. "That is true. Speaking of, I *want* to see what Bloomingdale's has on sale." I pull Alex into the store and head for the dress section.

"What about this?" asks Alex, holding up a cute A-line dress with lots of flowers.

I shake my head no. "It's pretty, but too flowery for me. It's kind of a Nina dress."

Alex makes a face and puts the dress back on the rack. She slaps her forehead. "Oh! I forgot to tell you. She's been asking about you."

My stomach jumps. "What now? I thought she and I had moved on."

"I don't think it's bad. She said something about college applications. She seemed frazzled. Honestly, I kind of tuned her out."

I frown. "Nice, Alex. It wouldn't kill you to give her a chance, you know. People change."

Alex raises an eyebrow. "Says the girl whose first reaction was 'what now?' when I mentioned Nina's name?"

I hold up my hands in surrender. "Fine, we'll both work harder at seeing the new Nina. I need to talk to her about the Winter Formal dresses anyway. I'm feeling a little overwhelmed. Those three days in LA really set me back. And then there's the portfolio stuff on top of that. Lots of pressure."

"You'll get it all done," Alex says confidently. She picks up another dress off the rack. It's a black, off-the-shoulder, A-line dress that goes down to mid calf. "This one is definitely you."

I love it. "It would look cute with my chunky black sandals."

"With this chain," says Alex, grabbing a silver necklace off a display.

"Done! Maybe this will be my outfit for Liesel's show," I say. "Jake got me a ticket."

"Maybe you can swing an extra ticket for your BFF?" Alex nudges me with her elbow.

I put my arm around her. "Not this time, I'm afraid. Besides, Jake and I have to talk."

"Riiight," says Alex. "Well, when you're famous, I expect to have a ticket to all your shows."

I pretend to think about it. "If you're lucky."

ALEX'S DRESS SHOPPING *Designs*

SWEETHEART NECKLINE

SKINNY STRAPS

PEACH & WHITE STRIPES

FULL SKIRT

BROWN SUEDE ANKLE BOOTS

PINK FLORAL PATTERN

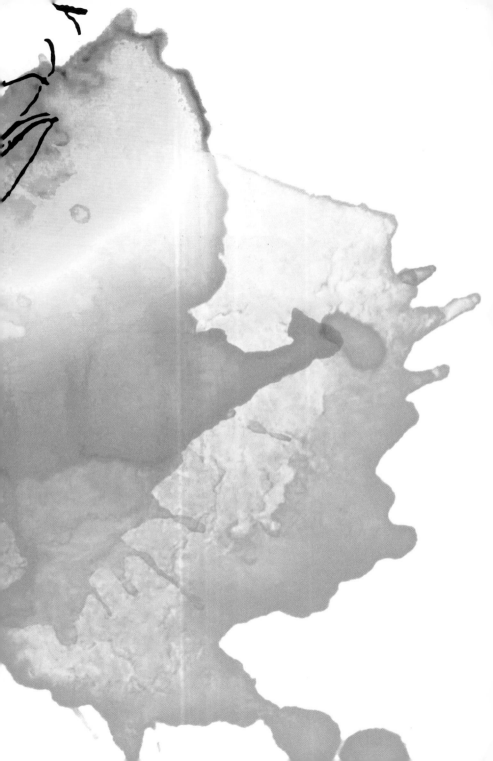

8

"Chloe!" Liesel exclaims when I arrive at the fashion show venue — an industrial-looking loft — on Saturday. "It's so wonderful to see you again!" She stops making last-minute adjustments on one of the models and hurries over to give me a quick hug.

"Same here," I say, hugging her back. "Thanks so much for inviting me. Jake said the theme is *biker ballerina*? That sounds so interesting! I'm not really sure what to expect."

"Well, I have to admit, I'm glad you can't quite picture it. That way when you see the designs you'll have an entirely fresh perspective."

I laugh. "Fair enough. Have you seen Jake? I'm supposed to be meeting him here."

As if on cue, Jake comes around a corner. When I see him, I can feel my whole face brighten, and I give him an excited wave. Jake grins and walks over, sweeping me up in a hug.

"I can't believe I'm finally seeing you in person!" he says when he pulls back.

I blush. "I know. It feels like it's been forever."

Just then the lights flash off and on. "Well, that's my cue," Liesel says. "You two better get to your seats. See you soon! Enjoy!"

Liesel hurries back to her models, and Jake takes my hand. My stomach gets butterflies. It's been so long since he's held my hand. The way we left things in New York was with the understanding that the time wasn't right for us then. But holding Jake's hand reminds me how much I've missed him.

We hurry to our front-row seats, and the spotlights surrounding the runway flash on. The audience quiets, and the music cues up. As soon as the first model steps onto the runway, I'm transported to the world of Liesel's fantastic designs. *Biker ballerina* turns out to be a combo of tough and feminine. It's such a great concept. All the designs have an element of leather, and the models' faces are stoic.

As cool as our high school's fashion show was, this is even better. There's pressure and tension in the air.

Photographers are snapping photos from the sides, and the front row is filled with reviewers. It's like the New York hype but in California. Not just in California, but in my hometown.

A model in a brown leather skirt with contrasting blue leather pockets struts down the runway. The skirt is paired with a tight, cropped sweater and black strappy sandals. I like the edginess of the look.

The next look is more monochromatic but equally chic. It's a black leather trapeze dress with contrasting piping on the collar and pockets. Liesel has it paired with sandals that lace up to the knee. The dress is both fierce and feminine.

The next model comes out in an outfit that I not only love but could see myself wearing too. It's white and taupe with dark blue accents and eyelet shoulder details. I like the striped pattern, and the blue is a fun, bright pop of color.

"You'd look nice in that," Jake whispers.

"Maybe your mom will give it to me as an early Christmas present," I joke.

"Well, you definitely have the right connections," Jake replies, giving my hand a squeeze.

More models come out, and I'm so impressed with Liesel's range. After she won *Design Diva* several seasons ago, she started a jewelry line. Then, when I was in New York, she collaborated with Stefan Meyers on his art deco

LIESEL'S FASHION SHOW *Designs*

MONOCHROMATIC

WHITE PIPING

CROPPED STRIPED SWEATER

BIG POCKETS

LEATHER COLOR-BLOCK SKIRT

LACE-UP STRAPPY HEELS

LEATHER & SUEDE

gowns. And, with this new collection, she's showcasing her eye for edgy, feminine style. When I did work for the PR department during my internship, I noticed how easy it was to identify the clothing of some designers. That's not the case with Liesel. It's like she's always reinventing herself. I want to be the same way. I want my designs to keep people guessing.

* * *

After the show, Jake and I congratulate his mom and then head back to my house. We sit on my porch swing. He hasn't let go of my hand since the show, and I'm glad.

"So it seems like you liked FIDM, huh?" he says softly.

I nod. "How did you know?"

"I'm a smart college boy, remember. Not to mention that you managed to answer all of my texts except for the ones about FIDM." He smiles. "It was sort of a giveaway."

"Picked up on that, did you?"

Jake taps his temple with his finger. "Like I said, smart." We sit quietly for a few minutes, and then he says, "Tell me about the tour, Chloe. I want to hear about it. Seriously."

I smile. Jake is such a good guy. All he wants is for me to be happy. I take a deep breath and tell him all about the tour and the FIDM museum. I talk about the classrooms and how bright and colorful the walls are. I glance over at him when I'm finished and feel better when I see his wide smile.

"It sounds amazing," Jake says. "Now I wish *I* had looked into that school!"

I nod. "I'm glad I saw it. And I'm glad we went to the fashion show today. Both these things made me realize how much California has to offer. I think I kind of wrote it off since I grew up here. But now, even if I do choose New York, I'll at least feel like I gave both options a fair shot."

Jake nods. "That's all you can do. I mean, I'd obviously love it if you came to New York, but you have to do what's best for you."

While I'm in the middle of tackling topics that make me nervous, I might as well bite the bullet and ask Jake about Winter Formal too. "Um . . . I also wanted to ask you . . . there's a dance in December," I say. "I know it's a long shot, but do you want to go with me? I mean, that's if you're coming out to Cali to spend the holidays with your dad. Otherwise don't worry about it. I don't want to —"

Jake grins. "I thought you'd never ask," he interrupts.

I'm surprised. "How did you know?"

Jake blushes. "I saw Alex mention something about dresses you're designing for the dance online, and . . . I might have looked up your school's website to see when your winter break is. I am coming out here for the holidays, and I had to book my plane tickets and work out details with my dad. I saw the dance on the website. But you never mentioned it, so I didn't want to push. I thought maybe you wanted to go with someone else."

"Oh my gosh, no! I just didn't know if you'd be able to come." Talk about miscommunication. "Speaking of the dresses I'm designing, did you happen to see that Nina is helping me?"

Jake raises an eyebrow. "Nina? Apparently we have a lot of catching up to do."

"A lot," I say with a smile.

"Let's not get this behind again. I want to know what's going on with you. You can tell me anything."

I squeeze his hand. "Thanks. Same goes for you."

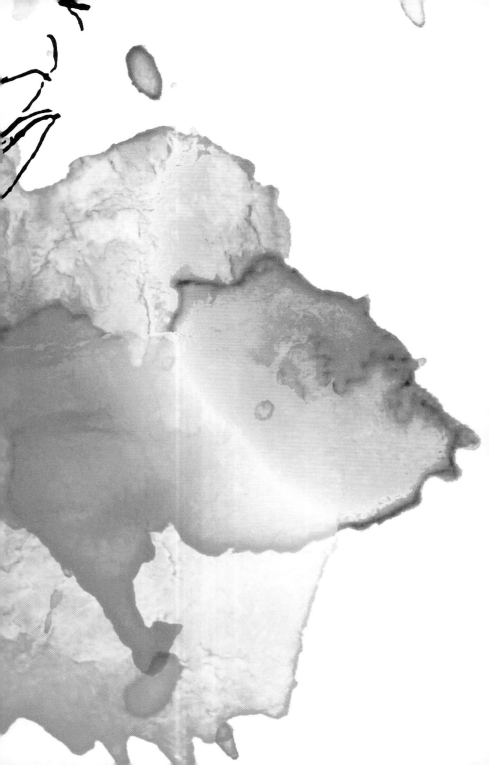

"My application is due November first," Jada, one of Alex's new friends, says at lunch on Monday, "and I don't think I can do it." Jada is applying early decision to Ivy League schools, so her applications are due almost two months before the rest of ours.

Mia, another of Alex's new friends, glances in my direction and shakes her head. Just two weeks ago, I didn't want to hear any college talk — it was too overwhelming. But since I've visited FIDM, I feel better about the whole process.

"Don't worry, Mia," I say. "I'm okay. Besides, if I had something due in two weeks I'd be a real mess."

"Thanks," Jada says with a groan.

"No, I mean I can't believe how well you're handling everything. You seem so calm," I say.

Jada laughs. "It's all on the outside."

"What do you have left to do?" Dan, Alex's boyfriend, asks. He and Alex are holding hands, as usual. Seeing them together bummed me out when I first came home since I missed Jake, but after this weekend, their lovey-dovey stuff just makes me smile.

Jada blushes. "Not much. Just sorting my files and uploading them to the right websites."

Mia rolls her eyes. "Sounds like you're done. What's freaking you out?"

"Well," I say, mock seriously, "attaching a document can be hard. What if Jada attaches a clip of puppies instead of her college essay?"

"Yeah," Alex jumps in, "imagine Yale opening the file, and it's a dog chasing a ball. Tricky stuff."

Jada throws a corn chip at Alex. "You guys are the worst!" she exclaims.

"Fine," I say, throwing a chip back at her. "What's really bothering you?"

Jada sighs. "It's kind of stupid, but sending everything in is just so *final*. Does that make sense?"

This time no one teases her. That's something we all get. Even Dan, who's normally goofy, looks a little sad.

"It completely makes sense," says Alex. "It's like we spend all this time working toward this huge thing, and then it's done. Then what?"

"And *then* we have to decide where to go," Mia says. "Ugh, I hate decisions."

"Okay, enough with the depressing big-decision talk," says Dan. "We have the rest of senior year to look forward to. Winter Formal, prom, graduation . . . once college applications are done, it's party time."

"That's another way to look at it," says Jada, smiling again. "Okay, you've convinced me. I'm going home today, attaching documents like crazy, and hitting send."

"That's what I'm talking about," says Dan. "Like a Band-Aid."

I take out my sketchpad to capture this moment of all of us together. I start drawing Alex, who's wearing black leggings, an oversized blouse, a brown scarf, and brown boots. Just last year, those boots would have been sneakers, and she'd never have worn a scarf as an accessory. Then I add Jada's preppier look to the page — a button-down shirt with the sleeves rolled up, blue shorts, and a brown belt.

"Do me next," says Mia, noticing my sketch. She sucks in her cheeks and strikes a pose.

I sketch Mia's ivory tulle skirt, chunky black ankle boots, fitted black shirt, and slouchy hat.

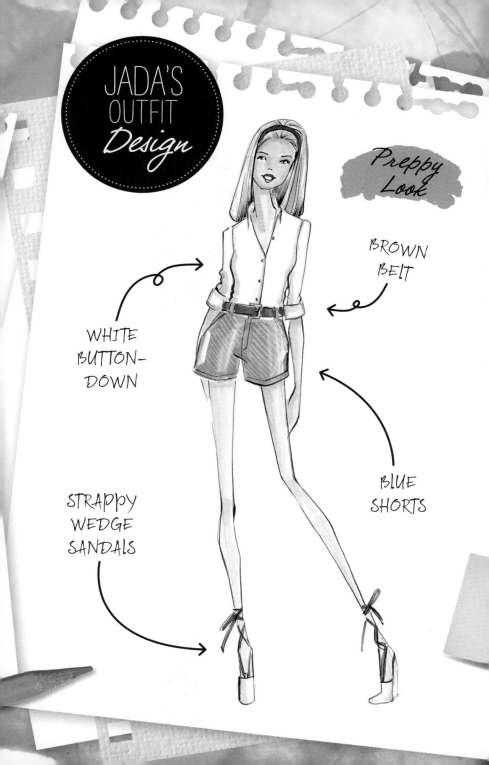

"Chloe, I'm taking you to New York with me," says Mia, leaning over to admire my finished drawing.

I pause. "You're applying to New York?"

Mia nods. "I just added NYU to my list. I decided I'm definitely majoring in theater, and they have a great program."

"That's great!" I say. I add a mental checkmark to the New York column. I could have another friend there too.

"Can we just pretend for a few minutes that there's no college stuff left to do?" says Jada. "Let's focus on some of that fun stuff Dan was talking about."

For the last few minutes left of lunch, I take Jada's cue. Even though I'm feeling better about my LA versus NYC decision and college stuff, I'd be lying if I said all those things weren't always in the back of my mind. But for now, I hug my friends and pretend none of us have anything left to worry about.

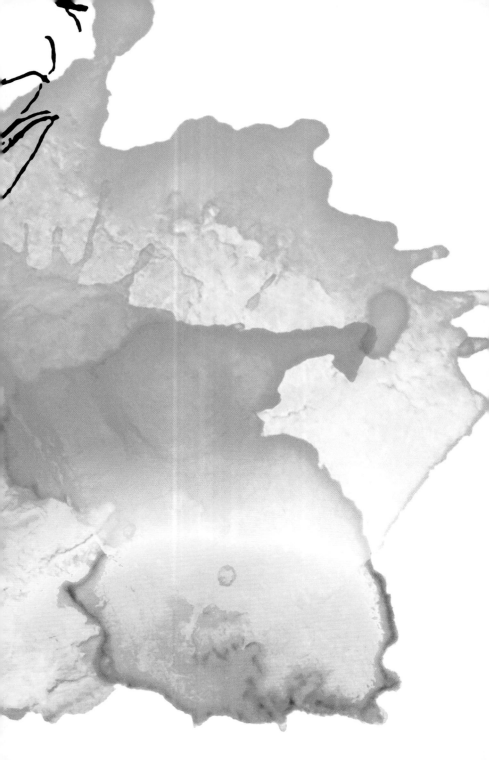

The next day at lunch, I'm sitting in the courtyard waiting for Nina. That morning she appeared at my locker, looking more stressed than I've ever seen her — even taking into account our time on *Teen Design Diva*. She asked if we could meet for lunch, and I agreed. Alex wasn't thrilled I'd be "ditching" her, but I'm hoping she doesn't really see things that way.

"Hey," says Nina, plopping down on the bench beside me. Her hair is all over the place, and her eyes look tired, but her outfit is as stylish as ever. Today, she's wearing a loose gray sweater and a floral skirt. "How was FIDM? We haven't had a chance to talk since you got back."

"It was fantastic," I reply. "I liked it way more than I was expecting to."

"Right? I was so impressed when I visited over the summer." Nina plays with the bracelet on her hand, opens her lunch, and frowns. "I'm not in a tuna mood. This morning I kind of was, but not now. You have to be in a tuna mood to eat it."

I take a bite of my turkey sandwich, not sure what to say. Nina seems all over the place. Tuna mood or not, she unwraps her sandwich and starts to eat. After she doesn't say anything for five minutes, I ask, "So, what's going on?"

Nina groans. "Sorry, I know I'm being weird. All this application stuff is starting to get to me. I know you felt behind because you hadn't visited schools or started your portfolio, but your real-world experience is kind of intimidating. I was thinking we could help each other."

I almost choke on my sandwich. It's one thing to not hate each other but help? "How would that work exactly?"

Nina looks down and takes a sip of her drink. "I know we weren't exactly friends before, and I —"

"Didn't always play fair?" I interrupt, thinking back to how Nina tried to sabotage me on *Teen Design Diva*.

Nina rolls her eyes. "Fine. Let's say that. But we also pushed each other. We got better because we both wanted to win so badly."

I also wanted to win *fairly*, but I don't harp on that. She's right in a way. I would have preferred Nina not be so obnoxious, but she did make me want to do my best. "Yeah, okay," I say.

"So, here's what I'm thinking — I'm probably ahead of you on the application front, but you can tell me a lot about working in the fashion industry and things you learned from your internship. If we work on our portfolios together, we can bounce ideas off each other." She pauses, puts her sandwich to the side, and picks up her apple.

It's not an idea I would have thought of myself, but it's a good one. I told Alex we need to try to see the new Nina. I'd be a hypocrite if I didn't take my own advice. Besides, it's not a competition like *Teen Design Diva*. If Nina gets into a design school, it doesn't mean I won't get into the same one. It's not really a rivalry anymore.

"Deal," I say.

Nina perks up, and she looks much more relaxed than when she first sat down. "There's only ten minutes left of lunch, but I brought some of my Winter Formal designs. I wanted to get your thoughts on them. Then maybe next week you can come over and show me yours and your portfolio too."

"Sounds good," I say as Nina opens her sketchpad.

She flips through the pages. Nina's designs are very pretty but understated. They have elements that stand out, but they're not big on embellishments. The first dress is a

- Textured Bodices
- Floral Accents
- Shades of Plum

NINA'S PORTFOLIO *Sketches*

FLOOR-LENGTH OMBRÉ GOWN

HALTER BALL GOWN

FLORAL ACCENTS

SILK FABRIC

COCKTAIL DRESS

Nina's Winter Formal ideas

PLUM-TO-WHITE OMBRÉ EFFECT

APPLIQUÉD FLOWERS

TEAMWORK: CHLOE & NINA COLLABORATION!!

A-LINE SKIRT

FLOOR-LENGTH GOWN

Winter Formal & Portfolio Requirements

floor-length ombré gown done in silk. Darker shades of plum start at the top and fade into white at the bottom. The bodice is textured and looks like a bunch of flowers sewn together.

I look through more of Nina's pages. Her dresses play with texture and most have a flower motif. I like the variations of floral designs. She even has a few with flowers delicately embroidered into the dress. One of my favorites, not surprisingly, is one without a floral print.

"That one's kind of plain, don't you think?" Nina asks, biting her lip.

I laugh. "I love it. I would totally wear it." The skirt is lavender and a wrap style, and the top is a perfect contrast in a darker purple. She paired it with open-toed shoes in a floral print, which helps break up the solid colors.

Nina laughs too. "I bet we can take each other out of our own comfort zones more."

By the time the lunch bell rings, Nina is smiling. I realize I am too and have been for most of lunch period. It's been a week of surprises. LA was as great as New York City. Talking with Jake wasn't as scary as I'd built it up to be. And now it seems I'm bonding with someone totally unexpected. Whatever happens next, I have a feeling there will be more surprises in store.

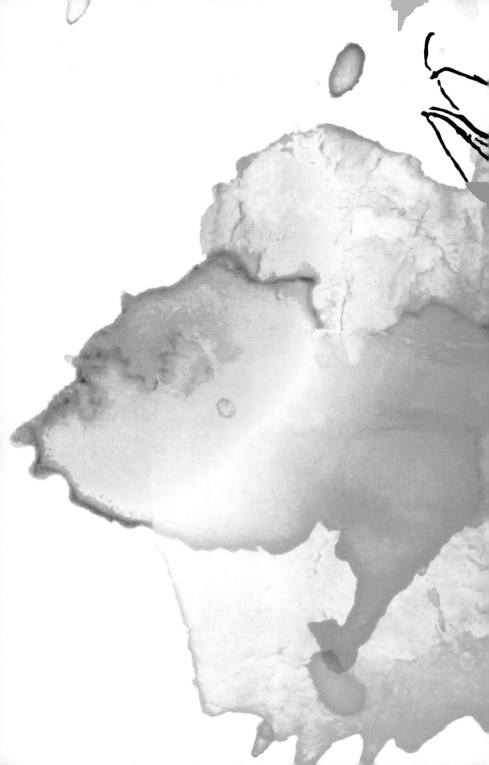

MARGIE

Author Bio

Margaret Gurevich has wanted to be a writer since second grade and has written for many magazines, including *Girls' Life*, *SELF*, and *Ladies' Home Journal*. Her first young adult novel, *Inconvenient*, was a Sydney Taylor Notable Book for Teens, and her second novel, *Pieces of Us*, garnered positive reviews from *Kirkus*, *VOYA*, and *Publishers Weekly*, which called it "painfully believable." When not writing, Margaret enjoys hiking, cooking, reading, watching too much television, and spending time with her husband and son.

BROOKE

Illustrator Bio

Brooke Hagel is a fashion illustrator based in New York City. While studying fashion design at the Fashion Institute of Technology, she began her career as an intern, working in the wardrobe department of *Sex and the City*, the design studios of Cynthia Rowley, and the production offices of *Saturday Night Live*. After graduating, Brooke began designing and styling for Hearst Magazines, contributing to *Harper's Bazaar*, *House Beautiful*, *Seventeen*, and *Esquire*. Brooke is now a successful illustrator with clients including *Vogue*, *Teen Vogue*, *InStyle*, Dior, Brian Atwood, Hugo Boss, Barbie, Gap, and Neutrogena.

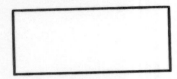